Willow in Africa

Contents

Chapter 1

Welcome to Africa

Willow stepped off the tiny plane on to the dusty orange ground. Everything looked different. Everything smelt different. It was much too hot. "I want to go home," Willow thought.

"Welcome to Africa!" A man was walking forward to greet them. "My name is Dion." Willow's mum shook Dion's hand.

"Nice to meet you," she said. "We're so excited to be here, aren't we, Willow?" But Willow just stared down at the floor, kicking at the dust.

The old jeep pulled up outside what looked like a tin shed. Willow groaned, "We are not going to live here!"
"Don't be silly," her mum said. "That's where the animals stay. We'll live in that lodge."
She pointed to a large brick building a little further down the dirt track.

Willow was pleased to see that at least this building had a roof and four walls. But that was about the only good thing she could say about it. The lodge looked like it could be knocked down by a light breeze.

Willow looked around the lodge. Inside was just as old and crumbly as the outside. Nothing like the modern city flat she used to live in. She couldn't see a TV anywhere. She got her mobile phone out to text her friends back home. There was no signal. How was she going to survive living here?

"I'm going to check on the animals. We can unpack later," Mum said, dumping their bags in the hall and picking up her medical kit. "Want to come?"

Willow shook her head. Her mum was a vet, but Willow had never been interested in animals. When she had decided to buy an old, run-down wildlife sanctuary in the middle of the Serengeti Willow's mum had been so excited.

"It will be great! A change is just what we need," she had said. "Think of how much more time we will have together. No more late nights at the office and takeaways. It will be just you and me and the animals."

Willow didn't share her mum's enthusiasm. She had to admit it would be nice to see her mum more. They had barely had any time together. But she liked living in the city. They had everything they needed there. She didn't want to move to some strange, new country full of scary animals where she didn't know anyone.

But once her mum had made up her mind, there was no changing it. And Willow had had no choice but to go, too.

Chapter 2

The New Arrival

Life at the lodge was worse than Willow had imagined. They were in the middle of nowhere, the nearest shop was miles away, and there was nobody around her own age. She couldn't even contact her friends back at home. She was stuck at the sanctuary with nothing but the boring animals for company.

It was hard work getting the animal sanctuary back up and running. The previous owners had abandoned it, and left it in a terrible state.

The sanctuary looked after sick and injured wild animals. This meant there was always a cage or stable that needed cleaning out, and water and food bowls that needed filling. Willow had hardly seen Mum since they'd arrived. She was always off in the barns with the animals, fixing broken stables, or discussing a case with Dion.

Willow groaned as her alarm went off ridiculously early.

"Come on, Willow," Mum called from downstairs. "Those animals won't clean their own enclosure."

"I wish they would," Willow grumbled to herself. She didn't understand why she had to spend all her time looking after these animals. It was Mum who had wanted to come here, not her. Willow lugged around bales of hay and buckets of water. It was tiring work.

"Don't put that there," Dion told her as she dumped a bag of pellets by the door.

Willow ignored him. This was Mum's sanctuary, not his. She could do what she liked.

Her mum came in and tripped over the bag of pellets. "Who put that there?" she sighed, dragging it out of the way.

Willow slipped out of the barn before she got told off.

When Willow was finally finished she went into the kitchen, hot, dirty, and starving. There she found Ada busy making breakfast. Ada placed a delicious plate of fresh fruit in front of Willow. "Mmm, thanks," Willow said, biting into a slice of juicy watermelon.

Ada looked after the lodge. She was the only good part about living here, as far as Willow was concerned. Willow had never known her grandparents, but Ada was exactly how Willow imagined a grandmother would be. She was kind, she didn't tell her what to do and, most importantly, she cooked the best food Willow had ever tasted. Much better than the takeaways she and her mum used to have almost every night.

Mum rushed in.

"Coffee?" Ada asked her.

"No time," Mum said. "We've got a new arrival. A baby giraffe. Sounds like it's been attacked by a lion."

Willow looked up, slightly interested. This was the first time they'd had an animal that big at the sanctuary.

"Willow, we need your help getting everything ready."

Willow moaned. A giraffe might be slightly more interesting than a warthog or a wild dog, but it was still just another animal, and Willow had only just sat down.

"I will bring Willow when she has finished her breakfast," said Ada.

Willow smiled at her gratefully.

13

When Willow went down to the sanctuary later, she found the baby giraffe lying on the hay. A huge cut had been patched up on his back leg. The giraffe's chest rose and fell heavily as he struggled to breathe. Willow didn't have to be a vet to know that he was very poorly. She didn't like seeing him lying there on his own. He was only a baby, after all.

She let herself into his enclosure. Kneeling down next to the poorly giraffe, she stroked his long neck. His hair was soft and smooth. The giraffe opened his huge eyes and stared up at Willow. He looked so sad.

"Please get better," Willow whispered. She leant down and kissed the giraffe on the neck.

"What are you doing in there?"
Willow jumped as Dion walked in. "You shouldn't be in there," he said. "Especially on your own. These aren't pets, they are wild animals. They could be dangerous."
"Alright, I'm sorry. Stop telling me what to do," Willow snapped, and she stomped out of the enclosure. What right did he have to tell her off? He wasn't in charge. She knew she wasn't supposed to go in with the animals by herself. But there was something about the giraffe. Willow shook her head. Why was she getting so soppy over an animal? This place was starting to get to her.

Chapter 3
Shadow

The next morning Willow was surprised to see the giraffe wandering around outside the lodge.

"Hey," she called. "What are you doing out here?" She was sure he should still be locked up in his enclosure. Mum liked to keep the animals in their pens while they recovered. He must have escaped.

The giraffe walked over to Willow. He hobbled slightly, but he was looking so much better. He was tall, and looked funny on his long gangly legs. He lowered his long neck down to Willow and licked her hair. Willow went to stroke him, but remembered the trouble she had got into the day before.

"I'd better find Mum," she said.

Willow looked around, but she couldn't find anyone. The giraffe followed, hobbling close behind her.

"Are you going to follow me everywhere? You're like my shadow," she said. "Hey, maybe that's what we should call you. Shadow!" He bent down and licked her hair again in reply.

Then Willow had an idea. "Come on," she said.

Willow walked towards the giraffe enclosure. As she expected, Shadow followed her all the way inside. "No more escaping," Willow told him, shutting the gate firmly behind her.

Just then, Mum and Dion came in.
"Willow, what are you doing in there? You know it's not safe!"

"But ..." Willow began.

"I thought you knew better than that," Mum said, angrily.
"I tried to tell her yesterday," Dion said.
They both looked cross.

Willow ran out of the enclosure. She wished
everyone would stop having a go at her.
She wished it was back to just being her and
her mum. She wished they had never come.

Willow's mum found her hiding in the food shed.
"I was just trying to help," Willow said, tears running
down her face. "Why did Dion have to get cross?
It's got nothing to do with him."

"Dion is just trying to help. He knows more about the wildlife here than anybody. We could never have got this place up and running without him. You should give him a chance. This is our home now. It might be nice to have some friends."

Mum gave her a hug. "I'm sorry I didn't trust you. And I know I've been busy, but it will get better. How would you like to come and help feed the baby giraffe now?"

Willow nodded. As soon as Shadow saw Willow again, he came straight over. Willow held up a carrot, and he took it from her hand. "He likes you. He won't feed from anyone else," said Mum. Willow smiled. She liked him too.

"We should be able to release him soon," said Mum.

Willow's heart sank. "But he's only just got here!

Why can't he stay? I'll look after him."

"He needs to go home, to be with his own kind.

His mum will be missing him."

Willow looked up at the beautiful giraffe. She knew

how it must feel for him to be in a strange new

place, away from his home. But she didn't want him

to go. Just when she was starting to feel like she had

finally made a friend here.

Over the next few days, Shadow got stronger and stronger. He ran around the paddock happily. Whenever Willow went outside, he came straight over to say hello with a lick and a nuzzle. Willow found herself spending all of her free time with Shadow.

But all too soon it was time for Shadow to be released back into the wild.

"I don't want him to go," Willow told her mum.

"I know it's hard, but he belongs in the wild with his own kind," Mum said.

Willow understood, but it didn't make it any easier.

"You can come with us if you want, and see where he lives," Dion said.

Willow shook her head and looked up at Shadow. He leant down and licked her hair the way he always did. How could Willow ever say goodbye? It was too hard.

Chapter 4
Home

The sanctuary didn't feel the same without Shadow. Willow missed him more than anything. Even Ada's delicious baked treats weren't enough to cheer Willow up.

"We're releasing some of the warthogs tomorrow," Dion told Willow. "I thought you might like to come this time. It will be good for you to see how happy they are in the wild."

Willow shrugged.

"It's beautiful out there. You'll enjoy it, I promise," Dion said, smiling at her.

Willow thought about what her mum would say. Maybe she should give Dion a chance. It wouldn't hurt to have a few friends out here, especially now Shadow was gone. "Okay," she finally agreed.

The next day, Willow helped Dion catch the warthogs and load them into the truck. "We want to find a nice spot for them. Somewhere near a waterhole, with plenty of vegetation, and as far away from people as possible," Dion explained. "Let me know if you see anywhere that looks good." Willow felt pleased that Dion wanted her choose where to release them.

They drove for miles until they came to a beautiful spot. It was flat and shrubby. It looked perfect for a warthog.

"What about here?" Willow said, hoping Dion would agree. Dion stopped and looked around.

"It looks perfect," he said. Dion and Willow opened up the cage. The warthogs ran around, squealing happily, sniffing their new home.

"I think they like it. You made a good choice," Dion smiled.

Willow laughed. Dion was right, they did look happy. And it was nice to see them out in the wild. Willow wished she had seen Shadow being released, too.

The sun began to go down. Lots of animals started to come out in the cool evening. Willow didn't want to go back to the lodge yet. She could have stayed out here forever, watching the sunset. Luckily, Dion wasn't in any hurry to go back either. They sat in silence, watching the wildlife. Willow wondered where Shadow was right now.

Then Willow gasped. A whole family of giraffes walked right past their jeep. Then a smaller giraffe appeared. Willow recognised him straight away. It was Shadow. And Shadow recognised Willow too. As soon as he saw her he came straight over. He nuzzled her hair like he always did.

Dion smiled at her, pleased that his plan had worked. Willow realised that this was why he had been so keen for her to come. "Thank you," she said to him.

Willow and Dion stayed and watched Shadow and his family until it was almost too dark to see. It was so nice to see the baby giraffe running through the long grass with his family and eating from the tall trees. His mother fussed over him, happy to have him back. Willow could see that he was in the right place. He was free.

And for the first time, Willow felt like she was in the right place too. She loved how quiet and peaceful it was here. She couldn't imagine going back to the city now – it would be like going into captivity. Out here for the first time she felt free, she had friends, she even felt like she had a family.

Willow realised that, just like Shadow, perhaps she belonged in the wild, too.

Things to think about

1. How does Willow feel about going to Africa?
2. Why does Willow find it hard to adjust to being in such a different place?
3. How is Willow's relationship with her mum affected?
4. What effect does caring for Shadow have on Willow?
5. How does Willow feel at the end of the story? Why? How would you feel if you were Willow?

Write it yourself

This story explores how people feel when they go to a new, unfamilar place and the struggles they may have. It also shows how different can be good. Now try to write your own story with a similar aim. Plan your story before you begin to write it.

Start off with a story map:

• a beginning to introduce the characters and where and when your story is set (the setting);

• a problem which the main characters will need to fix in the story;

• an ending where the problems are resolved.

Get writing! Think carefully about contrasts in your story. What sort of changes are involved? What is given up? What is gained? Is there a lesson learnt at the end?

Notes for parents and carers

Independent reading

The aim of independent reading is to read this book with ease. This series is designed to provide an opportunity for your child to read for pleasure and enjoyment. These notes are written for you to help your child make the most of this book.

About the book

Willow is nervous about leaving her friends and familiar surroundings behind to go to a remote area of Africa. She misses her old way of life. But soon, she befriends an injured giraffe called Shadow and discovers how meaningful life at a wildlife sanctuary can be.

Before reading

Ask your child why they have selected this book. Look at the title and blurb together. What do they think it will be about? Do they think they will like it?

During reading

Encourage your child to read independently. If they get stuck on a longer word, remind them that they can find syllable chunks that can be sounded out from left to right. They can also read on in the sentence and think about what would make sense.

After reading

Support comprehension by talking about the story. What happened?
Then help your child think about the messages in the book that go beyond the story, using the questions on the page opposite. Give your child a chance to respond to the story, asking:
Did you enjoy the story and why? Who was your favourite character?
What was your favourite part? What did you expect to happen at the end?

Franklin Watts
First published in Great Britain in 2019
by The Watts Publishing Group

Copyright © The Watts Publishing Group 2019
All rights reserved.

Series Editors: Jackie Hamley and Melanie Palmer
Series Advisors: Dr Sue Bodman and Glen Franklin
Series Designer: Peter Scoulding

A CIP catalogue record for this book is
available from the British Library.

ISBN 978 1 4451 6517 2 (hbk)
ISBN 978 1 4451 6518 9 (pbk)
ISBN 978 1 4451 6937 8 (library ebook)

Printed in China

Franklin Watts
An imprint of
Hachette Children's Group
Part of The Watts Publishing Group
Carmelite House
50 Victoria Embankment
London EC4Y 0DZ

An Hachette UK Company
www.hachette.co.uk

www.franklinwatts.co.uk

FSC
www.fsc.org
MIX
Paper from
responsible sources
FSC® C104740